W9-BSK-646

This Storybook Belongs To
Princess

My Perfect Wedding

Cinderella's dreams were coming true at last! She had managed to race down the stairs just in time to let the Grand Duke place the glass slipper on her foot.

Now she and the Prince were going to be married, and a new life filled with happiness would soon begin.

But first there was a wedding to plan....

Prudence, her lady-in-waiting, was taking charge. She sat with Cinderella and read off a long list of preparations.

"Excuse me, Prudence," Cinderella said when Prudence paused for a moment. "Couldn't we just have a simple wedding?"

Prudence frowned. "Cinderella, now that you are going to be a princess, you must start thinking big!"

Later, Prudence arrived with the royal dressmaker and several wedding gowns. The first gown was covered with bows.

"Do you think you could design something...plainer?" Cinderella politely asked the royal dressmaker.

"Certainly not!" Prudence cut in. "Plain and princess do not go together!"

Next was the visit to the florist. Unfortunately, that wasn't much better. When Cinderella and Prudence arrived, the florist greeted them with…a bush! At least Cinderella thought it looked like one.

"This is lovely," she said, "but do you have something a bit smaller?"

"This is perfect," Prudence interrupted, taking the bouquet from Cinderella. "You just have to know how to carry it." She held the flowers out in front of her—and was stung by a bee!

That afternoon, the mice found Cinderella sitting alone. Prudence had gone to bed to nurse her bee sting.

"I'll just have to take care of the wedding plans myself," Cinderella said. "Now, what should I do first?"

"Who'sa comin', Cinderelly?" wondered Jaq.

"The guest list! Good idea, Jaq. Let's see. Of course, all of you are invited," Cinderella replied, gently patting the mice. "And, my Fairy Godmother…I wish she were here right now."

And almost as fast as Cinderella wished it, her Fairy Godmother appeared! After giving Cinderella a big hug, she said, "We'll plan an absolutely magical wedding for you, my dear. Now, when is it exactly?"

Gus counted on his fingers. "Tomorrow!" he announced.

"Oh, my goodness, child!" cried the Fairy Godmother.

"Lots ta do!" Jaq added. He and Gus unfurled Prudence's list for the Fairy Godmother to see.

"Well then, let's start at the beginning—with the dress!" the Fairy Godmother gushed. With a wave of her wand, she instantly adorned Cinderella in an elegant white gown. But the Fairy Godmother had forgotten the veil.

"It's lovely," Cinderella said, "but don't you think it needs..."

The Fairy Godmother wasn't listening. She was already working on the next item—invitations! In moments, hundreds of lovely pink cards sat in stacks around the room.

"Now we shall prepare the feast and make the cake!" she announced. "I want everything to be perfect!"

Cinderella changed her clothes and followed the Fairy Godmother to the royal kitchen. Meanwhile, the mice stayed behind, picking up where the Fairy Godmother had left off. Mary, Suzy, and Perla threaded needles, pulled out a box of tiny pearls, and began making a veil.

"Invite-tations!" Jaq instructed the other mice. He gave each an armload of cards to deliver throughout the kingdom. Unfortunately, they didn't get very far before their plans were spoiled by Pom-Pom!

"Whew! Close-a call!" said Jaq as he and Gus raced away from Pom-Pom. They caught up with Cinderella in the castle kitchen. The Fairy Godmother put them right to work helping to create a great big, fancy cake!

Cinderella tried to hide her disappointment. "Um...Prudence will love it," she said. "You know, I really should go see how she's feeling."

"Poor child," the Fairy Godmother said after Cinderella had left. "These wedding plans must be too much for her."

Jaq and Gus tugged at the Fairy Godmother's sleeve.

"Cinderelly likes smaller things," Jaq told her.

Gus pointed proudly to himself. "Like mice!"

All at once, the Fairy Godmother understood.

Later, in Cinderella's chamber, the Fairy Godmother took Cinderella's hand.

"I'm afraid I may have gotten a bit carried away, my dear," the Fairy Godmother confessed. "Now tell me, child, what would the wedding of your dreams be like?"

After listening attentively to Cinderella, the Fairy Godmother began to perform her magic. First she fixed the veil. Then she sent the invitations out the window to destinations near and far.

"Now let's cut that cake down to size," the Fairy Godmother said with a twinkle in her eye. But before they departed for the kitchen, Cinderella turned toward the kind-hearted mice.

"Thank you, my little friends," she said gratefully.

The next day, Cinderella looked lovely in her simple white gown, veil, and gloves.

But just as the King was about to escort her down the aisle, Cinderella looked down and gave a little cry of surprise.

The Fairy Godmother followed the bride's gaze.

"Good heavens, child!" she exclaimed. "You can't get married in your bare feet!" She waved her wand, and Cinderella's beautiful glass slippers peeked out from underneath her gown.

After the ceremony, the Prince and Cinderella shared a joyous celebration with their guests. Even Prudence was pleased.

"However did you manage this?" the Prince asked his new princess.

Cinderella smiled and said, "With friends by your side, anything is possible!"